ALOE VERA MEDICINE

Medicines Of The Prophet

SHUAIBU ABDULLAHI

ISBN: 9798354538942

NAMES
1. IN HADEES IT IS CALLED AS SABIR (صبر).
2. IN HINDI & URDU IT IS CALLED AS GHIKAWAR
OR GUARPATHA.

3. IN ENGLISH & LATIN IT IS CALLED AS ALOE
VERA.

4. IN MARATHI IT IS CALLED AS KORPHOD.

5. ITS FAMILY IS XANTHORRHOEACEAE.

CONTENTS

PROPHET

NABI صلى الله عليه وسلمS GUIDANCE ABOUT SABIR (صبر) (ALOE VERA) ARABIC WORDS WRITTEN IN BELOW REFERENCES ARE THE WORDS MENTIONED IN RESPECTED HADEES. YOU CAN CONFIRM THE REFERENCES OF HADEES AT SUNNA.COM & AL-MAKTAB AL-SHAMILAH (المكتبة الشاملة)

TWO BITTER THINGS
1. HAZRAT QAIS IBN RAF'E رضي الله عنه SAYS THAT RASOOL ALLAH صلى الله عليه وسلم SAID "DO YOU KNOW WHAT CURE THE TWO BITTER REMEDIES HAVE CARRIES, ESHEEH (CRESS) & SABIR (صبر) (ALOE VERA.) : REFERENCE AL-HAAWI AL-KABEER VOLUME NO. 3; PAGE NO. 640.

Use **SABIR (Aloe Vera) for face brightness**

2. HAZRAT UMME Salma رضي الله عنها says that "When Abu Salma died, I had applied SABIR (Aloe Vera) on my eyes, and RASOOL Allah صلى الله عليه وسلم came & asked her "What is this, UMME Salma"? HAZRAT UMME Salma رضي الله عنها answered, "It is SABIR (صبر), it has no perfume in it, RASOOL Allah صلى الله عليه وسلم answered that "It makes the face Brighter, but do not use it expect Nights & remove it in day time, & do

not apply perfume when combing your hairs, or HEENA, because it is dye, Than HAZRAT UMME Salma رضـي الله عنها asked What should I use while combing my hairs oh! RASOOL Allah صلى الله عليه وسلم RASOOL Allah صلى الله عليه وسلم replied "Use Lotus leaves, to cover your head". : Reference Abu DAWUD: 2305; Book no. 13; In English Book no. 12; HADEES no. 2298.

SABIR (Aloe Vera) for eye infection

3. HAZRAT NUBAYH IBN WABH رضي الله عنه says that HAZRAT UMER IBN UDAIDULLAH IBN MA'MAR رضي الله عنه had an eye infection & he wanted to apply SURMA (kohl) in his eye, but HAZRAT ABAAN IBN Usman رضي الله عنه told him not to do so, & asked to apply SABIR (صبر) (Aloe Vera) in his eye, & said that he heard from HAZRAT Usman IBN AFFAN رضي الله عنه that, NABI صلى الله عليه وسلم did the same.

: Reference Abu DAWUD: 1838; Book no. 11; In English Book no. 10; HADEES no. 1834.

4. HAZRAT IBN Bin Usman narrates that his father رضي الله عنه says that one man had an infection in his eyes, while he was in Ihram & NABI صلى الله عليه وسلم advised him to apply SABIR (صبر) (Aloe Vera). : Reference An-NASA'I: 2711; Book no. 24; In English volume no. 3; Book 24, HADEES no 2712.

Uses of it

1. It can be taken orally as its natural Juice.

2. Apply on skin, wounds, ulcers, burns & etc.

3. Taken mix with medicines.

4. Taken in medicinal preparations.

Available in market as

1. Juice (in Natural form).
2. As shampoo, facc wash, gel to apply on face or hairs.
3. Ointments creams, etc.
4. Pickle.
5. Tablets, capsules (in dried form or its extract).
6. Oils.
7. As a gel to apply on the body.

Contents of it:

– it contains 200 active components & some are
carbohydrate, fats, steroids, copper, sodium, potassium, SULPHUR, protein, amino acids, unsaturated components, organic acids, iron, chloride, magnesium lactate, anti-prostaglandins, vitamin B1, B2, B3, B6, B12,calcium, manganese, digestive properties, cardio protective properties, skin protective properties & e t c

Scientific benefits of it

1. It helps in constipation (Because it is laxative).

2. Best to apply on cold sores, herpes zoster, herpes simplex, itching, ulcers, burns, viral infections, psoriasis.

3. Helpful in all types of cancers, skin cancers, jaundice, gall stone, HIV, diabetes, dry skin, frost bites, gingivitis.

4. Reduces cholesterol, inflammation, swelling, bed sores, dandruff, colitis, gastric ulcers.

5. Best if applied in burns, wounds, chronic ulcers, eye infections & etc.

6. Increases complexion & best in all skin problems.

7. HELFUL is all types of eye & skin diseases.

Contraindications

1. Motions, Diarrhea.
2. Pregnancy.
3. Vaginal BLEEDINGS

SCIENCE & HADEES
Regarding Aloe Vera: –

For eyes infection

It is a best home remedy for eyes infection of all types, because it has Antibacterial activity & properties.
Antibacterial: –
The activity of Aloe Vera inner gel against both Gram-positive and Gram-negative bacteria has been demonstrated by several different methods. Streptococcus PYOGENES and Streptococcus FAECALIS are two microorganisms

that have been inhibited by Aloe Vera gel. Aloe Vera gel reportedly was bactericidal against Pseudomonas AERUGINOSA while ACEMANNAN prevented it from adhering to human lung epithelial cells in a monolayer culture.

<u>ANTIFUNGAL</u>

A PROCESSED ALOE VERA GEL PREPARATION REPORTEDLY INHIBITED THE GROWTH OF CANDIDA ALBICANS.

Antiviral effects

This action may be direct and indirect. Indirect due to stimulation of immune system and direct is due to ATHRA Quinones. The anthrax Quinones ALOIN activates various enveloped virus; herpes simplex, varicella zoster (mainly eyes related) and influenza

Skin hydration actions

MUCOPOLYSSACARIDES help in binding moisture into the skin. It was proposed that the Aloe Vera gel containing products improved skin hydration possibly by means of a humectant mechanism.

Anti-aging effect

Aloe stimulates fibroblast which produces the collagen and elastin FIBRES making the skin more elastic and less wrinkled.

Wound-healing effects

Different mechanisms have been proposed for the wound-healing effects of aloe gel, which include keeping the wound moist, increase epithelial cell migration, more rapid maturation of collagen and reduction in inflammation.

GLUCOMANNAN, a mannose-rich polysaccharide and gibberellin, a growth hormone, interacts with growth factor receptor on the fibroblast, thereby stimulating its activity and proliferation, which in turn increases collagen synthesis after topical and oral application. An increase in synthesis of hyaluronic acid and DERMATAN sulfate in the granulation tissue of a healing wound is seen following oral and topical treatment.

Aloe Vera gel contains a glycoprotein with cell proliferating promoting activity, while in one research it is found that Aloe Vera gel improved wound healing by increasing blood supply, which increased oxygenation as a result. Topical application of the Aloe Vera derived ALLANTION gel stimulated fibroblast activity and collagen proliferation.

<u>Anti-inflammatory effects</u>

It inhibits the CYCLOXIGEANASE pathway and reduces prostaglandin E2. Recently, the novel anti-inflammatory compound called C-GLYCOSYL CHROMONE was isolated from gel extracts.

Recently, the peptidase BRADKINASE was isolated from aloe and shown to break down the BRADYKININ, an inflammatory substance that induces pain.

<u>Effect on immune system</u>

IMMUNO modulating effects occur via activation of macrophage cells to generate nitric oxide, secrete cytokines (e.g., tumor necrosis factor-α, interleukin-1, interleukin-6 and interferon-γ) and present cell surface markers.

<u>Antioxidant property</u>

Glutathione peroxides activity, superoxide dismutase enzymes and a phenolic antioxidant were found to be present in Aloe Vera gel, which may be responsible for these antioxidant effects.

<u>Antitumor effect</u>

The two fractions from aloes that are claimed to have anticancer effects include glycoproteins (LECTINs) and polysaccharides.

Different studies indicated antitumor activity for Aloe Vera gel in terms of reduced tumor burden, tumor shrinkage, tumor necrosis and prolonged survival rates. An induction of glutathione S-TRANSFERASE and an inhibition of the tumor-promoting effect of PHORBOL MYRISTIC acetate has also been reported which suggest aloe gel in cancer chemoprevention. Indirect action on antitumor activity is stimulation of the immune response

Laxative effect (Purgative effect)

ANTHRA Quinones increase intestine water content, stimulate water secretion and increase intestinal PERISTALIASIS.

Antiseptic   Properties
Aloe Vera contain six antiseptic agent; LUPEOL, salicylic acid, urea nitrogen, CINNAMONIC acid, phenol and sulfur.

Use of aloe Vera in dentistry
APTHOUS ulcer: –

It has been reported that ACEMANNAN hydrogel accelerates the healing of APTHOUS ulcers and reduces the pain associated with them. Researchers evaluated a gel that combined ALLANTION, Aloe Vera, and silicon dioxide and its effects on APTHOUS ulcers of the oral cavity. Each patient used a daily diary to document the number and duration of APTHOUS ulcers, the interval between ulcers, ulcer size, and ulcer pain over a period of 3-4 months.

The reduced duration of the lesions in one arm of the study and the increased interval between lesions in the other arm of the study both were significant statistically.

The gel did not demonstrate any consistent effectiveness on ulcers in the oral cavity.

ORAL LICHEN PLANUS

A patient of lichen PLANUS with systemic involvement placed on Aloe Vera therapy. The patient's treatment involved drinking 2.0 ounces of stabilized Aloe Vera juice daily for 3 months, topical application using Aloe Vera lip balm and aloe cream for itching hands.

The oral lesions cleared up within 4 weeks, although the systemic lesions took longer, due in part to the fact that the patient temporarily interrupted the course of aloe therapy and sought an alternate source of treatment.

The 46 patients with OLP were randomly divided into 2 groups.

Each group was treated with Aloe Vera mouthwash and triamcinolone ACETONIDE 0.1% (TA).

The treatment period for both groups was 4 weeks.

Patients were evaluated on days 8, 16 and after completing the course of treatment (visit 1-3). The last follow-up was 2 months after the start of treatment (visit 4).

Aloe Vera mouthwash is an effective substitute for TA in the treatment of OLP.

A double-blind trial on 54 patients was randomized into two groups to receive Aloe Vera gel or placebo for 8 weeks. The most common site of OLP was the lower lip. 81% patients treated with Aloe Vera had a good response after 8 weeks of treatment, while 4% placebo-treated patients had a similar response (P < 0.001).

Furthermore, 7% patients treated with Aloe Vera had a complete clinical remission. Burning pain completely disappeared in 33% patients treated with Aloe Vera and in 4% treated with placebo (P = 0.005). Therefore, Aloe Vera gel can be considered a safe alternative treatment for patients with OLP.

Another double-blind study of 64 patients with OLP were randomized to either Aloe Vera (32 patients) or placebo (32 patients), at a dose of 0.4 ml (70% concentration) three times a day. The patients were evaluated after 6 and 12 weeks. In the Aloe Vera group, complete pain remission was achieved in 31.2% of the cases after 6 weeks, and in 61% after 12 weeks. In the placebo group, these percentages were 17.2% and 41.6%, respectively.

Concluded that Aloe Vera improves the total quality of life score in patients with OLP.

<u>Gingival</u>

Aloe Vera gel reportedly has been used to treat gingivitis and has been effective against herpes simplex viruses.

ACEMANNAN, a prominent GLUCOMANNAN-stimulate gingival fibroblast proliferation.

<u>Pulp</u>

ACEMANNAM promotes dentin formation by stimulating primary human dental pulp cell proliferation, differentiation, extracellular matrix formation, and mineralization. ACEMANNAN also has pulpal biocompatibility and promotes soft tissue organization.

<u>Bacteria</u>

Results showed that Aloe Vera tooth gel and

the toothpastes were equally effective against C. ALBICANs, Streptococcus MUTANS, Lactobacillus acidophilus, Enterococcus FAECALIS, PREVOTELLA INTERMADIA, and PEPTOSTREPTOCOCCUS ANAEROBIUS. Aloe Vera tooth gel demonstrated enhanced antibacterial effect against S. MITIs.

<u>Extracted socket</u>

SALICEPT Patch (a freeze-dried PLEDGET that contains ACEMANNAN Hydrogel) significantly (P ` 0.0001) reduces the incidence of Alveolar OSTITIS compared with clindamycin-soaked GELFOAM.

<u>Denture adhesive</u>

Because of the sticky and viscous nature of ACEMANNAN, a prototype ACEMANNAN was formulated into a denture adhesive and evaluated for adhesive strength in both wet and dry conditions; the adhesive was also used to evaluate cytotoxicity to human gingival fibroblasts.

<u>Conclusion</u>

Aloe Vera is best for eye infections, it increases complexion but should be applied at night only and wash out in day, can be applied in IHRAAM, or anyone dead in family because it has no smell in it.

AUTHOR

BY   SHUAIBU ABDULLAHI